# The Twins, the Ghost and the Castle

Pau...

Illustrated by ...ie Phillips

A & C BLACK
AN IMPRINT OF BLOOMSBURY
LONDON NEW DELHI NEW YORK SYDNEY

For Joan and David

First published 2013 by A & C Black,
an imprint of Bloomsbury Publishing Plc
50 Bedford Square
London WC1B 3DP

www.bloomsbury.com

ISBN 978-1-4081-7626-9

A CIP catalogue for this book is available from the British Library.

Printed and Bound by CPI Group (UK) Ltd, Croydon CR0 4YY

3 5 7 9 10 8 6 4

# Contents

# Contents

# Chapter One

# The castle

On the outskirts of a seaside town, right next to the beach, there is a mighty castle facing the sea. On a clear day if you stand at the water's edge, you can see the shadow of the continent in the distance. It really is that close, which is probably why Henry the Eighth built the castle there in the first place – to keep out any nasty invaders. (If there was anyone being nasty in England, thought Henry, then it was going to be him alone.)

So, for nearly five hundred years the castle has been guarding the beach, and its grey stone ramparts are as strong and solid as the day it was first built. It has a deep moat lined with high, mossy walls, cannons bristling in all sorts of directions, and a tall white pole on which flutters a proud flag. Around the castle there are acres and acres of the most wonderful gardens and woods. If you hover above the fortress in a helicopter (and you won't catch me in one of those things), it looks like a Tudor rose: made up of four half-circle towers around a circular keep in the middle. (A keep is the stronghold of the castle, right in the centre. And in the bottom of the keep is the castle well – which gives you some idea just how important it is to have water to drink.) To get in you have to clomp across a heavy, wooden drawbridge and pass through the gatehouse.

The heroes of this story, however, weren't anywhere near the drawbridge. They were hiding in the bushes by the gardens looking for a way to sneak in. To buy an entrance ticket costs money, and Stella and Tom didn't have any money. In fact the twins had nothing at all to their name except the clothes on their backs, and those were grey and scratchy and joyless.

Stella and Tom were totally alone in the world without anyone to look after them. We shan't discuss how they came to be so alone and without their parents, and why they were running away, as that would be completely grim, and this is meant to be a happy story.

Perhaps…

The castle towered above them, immense and cold, and, peeking through the bushes, they both felt very small and insignificant.

'Do you really think we ought to?' asked Stella. 'I mean, sneak in round the back.' She looked worried.

Tom gave his sister a hug. Stella was a bright and clever girl, who drew the most amazing pictures of imaginary underground kingdoms, and Tom loved her more than anything else in the world. It broke his heart to see her unhappy.

He smiled at her. 'It is a bit naughty, but we shan't cause any trouble, and perhaps we could help by picking up some litter or something. Besides we won't be staying for long.'

'I can't wait to see what it looks like inside. Do you think there's a dungeon?'

'Probably loads,' said Tom. 'You know what kings are like, always clapping prisoners in irons and throwing them into jail.'

'If we get found out, do you reckon we'd get thrown in the dungeon?'

'Nah,' Tom chuckled. 'Anyway, they'll have to catch us first.'

He lifted up a bit of the thin wire fence, making a gap. 'Come on, in you go.'

The twins managed to get through the fence, and found themselves on the edge of the kitchen gardens, between the greenhouse and the cabbage patch. Not far away was a little cottage, probably the caretaker's.

The twins hid inside the greenhouse amongst the palm trees and waited to see if anyone was coming. When they were sure they were alone, they crept out and headed down the path towards the castle.

'We should walk slowly,' said Stella with a smile, 'that way we don't look suspicious. And if anyone asks, we just tell them our parents are in the garden.'

Tom grinned at her. Was Stella getting her spark back?

They walked down the garden path and over the bridge that crossed the moat at the back of the castle. There was a courtyard in the middle of the fortress and they found some stairs leading up to the battlements.

'Let's go up there,' said Stella. 'I have to climb on one of those cannons! And from up high we can get a good look.'

The castle was everything they had hoped it would be. Sitting on top of one of the big guns in the sun, you could see across the moat to the great gardens, the sea, and even France in the distance. Behind them were sets of windows and glass doors leading to the stately rooms. Though the inside of the castle looked inviting, as it was such a lovely day Stella and Tom decided to go back and explore the grounds first.

They ran around the main garden with its giant trees and long, grassy meadows. Some families had laid out picnic blankets and were lounging in the sun. Next to the lawn was another garden that had a big, rectangular pond running down the centre of it. The pond was full of carp whose scales flashed in the light. They tried counting them, but there were too many, and the fish kept hiding under lily pads.

The twins were feeling hungry by this point, and went to the kitchen gardens. Earlier they had passed some apple trees heavy with fruit – the ground below was piled high with them. The label on one of the trees said 'Newton Wonders'.

'I wonder if these are the sort that fell on his head,' asked Stella in between mouthfuls.

'Whose head?'

'Sir Isaac Newton – the man who discovered gravity when an apple dropped on his nut.'

'Oh yeah, I knew that.'

'You don't know anything,' Stella teased.

'I know I can beat you to the end of those woods,' said Tom, bolting off down the path. Stella chased after him.

They ran through the trees, Stella a little way behind Tom. From in here, the trees were so thick you couldn't see the castle at all. They stopped and listened to the creaking of the branches and the calling of the birds.

'How about we pretend we're in a fairy tale?' said Stella. 'We're lost in the wood a long way from home...'

'And then we find a path and come across an enchanted castle,' Tom added.

With that, they found the path again where it looped through the woods, and raced back to the castle, past fields of purple crocuses straining for the sun, and a statue of the god Mercury standing in the paddock with his winged sandals.

# CHAPTER TWO

# 'You can't be serious!'

The inside of the castle was like nothing they had seen before. (And having lived pretty much their entire lives without a real home, you can imagine what the grand rooms of a castle might have seemed like to them.) It wasn't a draughty, freezing sort of a castle – though it did have some dungeons – but more like a stately home.

There were quite a few rooms – the bedrooms each had a four-poster bed, and the elegant dining room had places set for twelve. There was a painted blue hallway with a glass domed ceiling in the centre of it, and several different sitting rooms with antique furniture. The walls were hung with gold-framed portraits of annoyed-looking men in white wigs (and you'd probably be annoyed too if you had to wear a scratchy hamster on your head).

12

Indian carpets lined the wooden floors; there were statues and chandeliers everywhere.

'Wow,' whistled Tom. 'What a place.'

Stella was staring at a glass case in one of the smaller rooms that had been set up a bit like a museum. The case had some brightly coloured military jackets, fancy hats, and a pair of shiny black boots. 'Look, Tom,' she said in a hushed voice. 'Real Wellington boots!'

Tom read the card: '"The famous boots, designed and worn by Arthur Wellesley, the Duke of Wellington, hero of the battle of Waterloo." This used to be his home,' said Tom. 'The Duke of Wellington's.' He shook his head. 'I wish it were our home.'

Stella looked around the room and thought for a moment. 'Well, why don't we *make* it our home then?' She shrugged her shoulders. 'If we're clever about it, and find good places to hide, no-one need ever know we're here. It's big enough, after all.'

'You can't be serious!' Tom laughed.

'Perfectly serious,' said Stella.

And he could see that she was.

The first thing they had to do was to find somewhere to hide. It had to be somewhere quite secret but comfortable. Like their own little mouse hole. After walking through the castle from top to bottom again, they found a little stairway off one of the landings that they hadn't noticed before. The staircase had a purple rope across the front of it. The sign said: 'No admission, Lord Warden's apartments.' They checked the guidebook in the gift shop. It turned out the castle was the Lord Warden's official residence, which he only used once a year.

'Let's have a peek,' said Tom.

When no one was looking, they ducked under the purple rope and tiptoed up the stairs. The Lord Warden's apartment looked very comfortable. It had a massive four-poster bed to sleep in, a bathroom with a deep, claw-foot bath, and a living room. The living room had lots of armchairs, books, board games and even a television. It had heavy red curtains that could be pulled shut, so even at night Stella and Tom wouldn't have to worry if someone could see the light.

'Perfect!' said Stella. 'We can hide here. They probably only check it once a day at closing time – if that.'

Sure enough at closing time they heard the sound of footsteps up the stairs. The twins quickly shuffled under the bed and held their breath.

A pair of shoes entered the room (attached, of course, to the legs and body of a castle keeper), clumped around a little, and then clumped out again.

Shortly after, the castle went silent. Through a crack in the curtains the twins saw the staff leave and get into their cars. All except one man who went round the back towards the cottage – probably the head caretaker.

The twins grinned at each other. They had done it.

* * *

The first few days of hiding away without getting caught were the trickiest, but after that, Stella and Tom got the hang of the place and how the staff worked – when they opened, when they cleaned, what time they went home in the evening.

They soon solved the problem of food. The castle had a café on the ground floor that served up cream teas, scones, sandwiches, fruit, crisps – you know the sort of thing. The cook prided herself on serving only the freshest of food, and so each afternoon she would throw out a perfectly good selection of things that had absolutely nothing wrong with them, apart from being a little stale.

The twins quickly worked out that if they could get hold of the bag before the rubbish was taken out then they could have as much food as they could eat. Carrot cake with lemon icing was Stella's favourite, while Tom liked bacon, lettuce and tomato sandwiches.

At bedtime, for pyjamas they borrowed some costumes from the gift shop that were printed like armour – which made them look like crusaders. They would then jump into their enormous bed and snuggle under the thick covers.

Each morning they would make the bed carefully, and put the room back exactly the way it had been the day before.

Not wanting to draw too much attention to themselves, the twins spent much of their day lounging in the apartment, playing games or reading books. When they felt like it, they could easily sneak outside to the gardens for a run around. They soon built a little, secret hut out of sticks in the wood which they christened 'Leafage'. It had a carpet of soft leaves for the floor, and little cushions made out of dried grass.

They were delightfully free. Free to do whatever they pleased, and with their very own home. Their very own castle.

But it wasn't before long, that they discovered they weren't the only ones hiding during the day, and coming out at night.

The castle had a secret.

They were not alone.

# CHAPTER THREE

# A deep, thunderous voice

One evening, after five o'clock when the staff had given the castle a last inspection and had gone home, Stella and Tom came out from hiding under their four-poster bed and went exploring, knowing that no-one would be back until eight the following morning.

'Tray race?' Tom suggested.

'You're on.'

They ran down the stairs, through the courtyard, and into the café. Grabbing two trays, they made their way back up to the main staircase, and placed them on the top of the landing. Then they stood at the far end of the corridor, near the dining room, feet behind an imaginary line.

'On your marks, set... go!' Tom shouted, and they were off, arms pumping, legs flying.

18

They reached the trays in a blur. Both twins leapt onto the plastic, crouching down, and the trays took off.

Down the stairs they flew, clattering loudly. Stella was in the lead, but only just – her tray totally out of control. She tried to take the turn down the stairs – wham! She was going too fast to make it. Stella collided with the wall side-on. Blam! Tom clattered into her. The marble bust on the recess above them wobbled, and shook, and wobbled… then stopped still.

'Owww!' Stella complained. 'Watch where you're going!'

'Watch where you're going yourself!' Tom groaned. Stella punched him on the arm, Tom hit her back. They glared at each other.

Then, from the top of the landing came a sound that sucked the breath out of their lungs, froze their limbs stiff, and sent a shock through them as if they had stuck their finger in a socket. It was a voice. A deep, thunderous voice. It boomed down from above, cutting through the air like a blade.

'You're lucky you didn't knock down that sculpture – break that, and the game would really be up!'

Stella and Tom yelped, hearts jolting.

Towering above them, his arms folded, his dark eyes piercing and cold, stood a ghost.

He stood there, just slightly flickering, his outline clear, the room behind visible through his body.

The ghost held himself proudly, chest out, poised. He had a shock of silvery-white hair. Silver sideburns crept across his cheeks towards a hawkish nose that dominated his face. He wore a dark jacket of an old-fashioned sort, with a white waistcoat, the buttons done up all the way to the top. Above the waistcoat was a smart cravat.

Stella and Tom couldn't speak. Their jaws hung down helplessly.

The ghost continued. 'That bust of my head was made by Turnerelli, the finest sculptor of his day.' He frowned. 'He sculpted kings and princesses, and I would be sad to see it broken.'

Tom managed to find some strength in his legs and stood up, keeping his eye on the ghost. He briefly turned and read the inscription on the base of the statue. His eyes widened. He looked down at Stella in amazement then back at the ghost.

'You're the Duke of Wellington,' he gasped.

The old man gave a snort. 'But of course I am.' He spread his arms wide. 'And this is my castle.'

Stella and Tom glanced at each other uneasily. Stella got to her feet and reached for her brother's hand. Both were trembling.

The Duke rubbed his chin while he looked them up and down. 'Hmmm,' he said. 'Now if you two have had enough of tray races for one evening, I've been meaning to have a talk with you. In my room, if you please.'

The ghost entered a doorway just off the landing. Tom and Stella stayed still, not brave enough to follow.

The Duke came back to the landing. 'Well, come on – I won't bite.' A hint of a smile passed over his lips. 'At least, I'll try not to.'

The Duke's room was sparsely furnished. One wall was lined with bookshelves, full of dusty books. There was a small pair of writing tables, and a large, oval-shaped window that faced out onto the moat. It was getting dark outside now. On one side of the room was an old camp bed with a faded blue cover, next to which was a high-backed armchair.

The Duke sat down in the armchair, disappearing into it a little bit, and told the twins to sit on the bed. The bed creaked, and felt like it was going to collapse.

'Don't worry about that old bed of mine, she's been on many a campaign with me and survived. Never could stand sleeping in those four-poster monstrosities like the one you use.'

'So, you know we've been staying here then?' Stella found her voice.

'Oh yes,' beamed the Duke. 'From the very first night you arrived.'

'Then why didn't you show yourself to us then?' Tom asked.

'And scare you off straight away?' The ghost wagged his finger. 'No, no, no. That wouldn't have done at all. A good soldier should always reconnoitre first before deciding on action, I learned that in India.'

'Recon-a-what?' asked Tom.

'Investigate. Scout. I needed to see what you were made of – whether you were good sorts. The sort of people I would be willing to have in my castle. Some of those tourists who come through here are quite rude.'

The Duke tried to drum his fingers on the armrests, but his fingers disappeared into the cloth so he stopped.

He looked down at his hands with a smile and a shake of his head.

'Even after all these years of haunting, I still can't get used to the fact that I can't really touch things.'

'And are we good sorts?' asked Stella, dreading the answer.

The Duke smiled. 'I'd say you were the very best sort,' he said. 'Your actions thus far speak of both courage and intelligence. But your stair riding leaves a lot to be desired.'

Stella and Tom smiled for the first time. They were slowly getting over the shock.

'What do you want of us?' said Stella.

'I'd like to see you stay, of course,' laughed the Duke. 'You have no idea how lonely it gets being stuck here all on my own. Besides,' he said, his dark eyes sparkling, 'I can see we're going to have lots of fun!'

# CHAPTER FOUR

# Hide and Seek

Though the Duke of Wellington, or the 'Iron Duke' as he was known, had earned a reputation in his life for being severe and strict, as he got older he had developed a soft spot for children and their games, and the years of being a lonely ghost had mellowed him further.

If you had the run of a real-life castle, and shared it with such a ghost, what do you think you would get up to? I'm sure you would come up with a whole list of fun things. I'll also bet that somewhere on that list is 'hide and seek'. It's obvious, isn't it?

The entire castle from the Lord Warden's rooms at the top, to the stone dungeons below, including the outside courtyards and the battlements, was 'in bounds'. (Being too large, the gardens weren't part of the game, and besides, the Duke couldn't appear there – he could only haunt the castle.) There were all the bedrooms to hide in. Queen Victoria's room had a massive wardrobe to climb into, and the bedrooms on the ground floor had desks to crawl under. There were plenty of thick curtains to sneak behind, and the carpets on the floors made it easy to pad around without being heard.

The game was most fun creeping around in the dead of night in pyjamas with torches. But the ghost kept on winning, being able to walk through walls and disappear into furniture, so they had to change the rules and he went into a bit of a sulk.

Tom's invention was a game called Snapping Crocodiles. It was a simple game. The entire living room floor area was a crocodile-infested swamp, and the only way to get around was by jumping from chair to chair. Fall in and you would be crocodile dinner. The twins bounced from chair to chair and laughed to see the Duke's legs sink into the sofa when he tried it.

One night they took apart the grandfather clock which had stopped, and, following the Duke's instructions, they put it back together again to make it work. The next day, the staff were completely startled and baffled when it started to chime loudly again, the first time it had done so in years.

When the nights got colder, they lit the gas fire and lay around it reading books, drinking hot chocolate, and eating toasted sandwiches. The Duke, being a ghost, didn't need to eat at all. But he was thrilled to have someone to take the books off the shelf and turn the pages for him, and he began re-reading his favourite books with all the enthusiasm of a child.

'Turn!' he would command, followed by, 'Thank you.' Stella and Tom took it in turns to be his book person. So if you could hear them as they sprawled on the floor on those evenings it sounded like: 'Munch, munch, slurp, slurp. Turn! Thank you. Munch, munch, slurp, slurp. Turn! Thank you,' and so on.

Stella discovered that the gift shop was now stocking pink princess costumes with tall hats and veils. She borrowed one, and it quickly became her favourite thing to wear. (She had never had dressing-up clothes before, so she had a lot of catching up to do.)

With Tom in his knight's pyjamas and Stella dressed like a queen, they turned the castle into a royal court, with the Duke as their best general, a part he played with some delight.

But perhaps their favourite thing of all was to be tucked up in bed, cosy and warm while the wind and rain howled off the sea and battered the windows, and listen as the Duke talked about his amazing life.

'Who was the toughest person you ever fought against?' asked Tom one evening.

The Duke thought for a moment. 'Hmm. Napoleon Bonaparte was perhaps my greatest adversary, but have you ever heard of Tipu Sultan, the Tiger of Mysore?'

The twins said they hadn't. 'Was he called the Tiger because he was fierce?' Tom asked.

'Fierce?' The Duke stopped and mimicked the cut and thrust of a sword. 'Oh yes, he was fierce alright. A bold warrior who fought the British many times. In his last battle he fought right till the end to defend his capital.'

'Was it you that killed him?' Stella wanted to know.

The Duke paused for a moment. 'No, he did not die by my hand. The battle had been raging for some time; we had bombarded Tipu's fortress something savage. His walls were already breached and the battle almost won before I found him, his sword still in his hand. The Tiger certainly roared to the last.' The Duke shook his head at the memory, his face serious. 'He wasn't one of those rulers who sit comfortable miles away and pretend to know what they're doing.'

'Then why did you fight him?'

The Duke sighed. 'The reasons why countries fight can be thorny. But for a soldier, the whole art of war consists in getting at what is on the other side of the hill. The British wanted to conquer

India, and Tipu Sultan stood in the way. Plain and simple.'

Stella and Tom thought about this for a moment. The Duke continued. 'And on the very afternoon we buried him, out of nowhere came the foulest, most ferocious storm I have ever encountered. It was the most unsettling thing.'

'Do you think the gods were angry that Tipu had been killed?'

'I don't know. Perhaps.' He looked reflective, then went on, 'I saw a marvel, though, Tipu's Tiger[1] – a wonderful toy from his palace. It's a large mechanical beast of a tiger, carved out of wood and painted with stripes. When you turn the handle it growls and bites with its jaws. And what do you suppose the tiger is biting?'

'A British soldier?' guessed Stella.

'Clever girl,' the Duke chuckled. 'A fierce plaything for a fierce ruler. Now off to sleep, both of you.'

---

[1] You can see Tipu's Tiger in the V&A Museum in London. It really is a clever thing.

# CHAPTER FIVE

# Harry Parkin

The head caretaker of the castle was Harry Parkin, known as 'Parky'. Parky was a large man, well over six feet tall, and the moth-eaten hat forever perched on his head made him look even taller. Parky had bristly eyebrows that rested above large, sad eyes; ears the size of small plates; and a nose that was quite broad and bulbous. His face hung down in folds and looked gloomy most of the time, and that's because he was.

Even though the other staff had worked for him for years, no one ever invited him to sit with them at tea to have a biscuit and a chat, and ask him about his news.

In truth, there wasn't much to tell. Looking after the castle was his whole life. And when Parky's work was done each day, he went home to the caretaker's cottage on the grounds near the woods, where he lived all by himself.

But because the castle was his life, it meant that Parky knew every corner of it, from top to bottom. And lately he was beginning to suspect that something was not quite right. He wasn't sure exactly, but he had the feeling that someone was doing something secretive about the place. That the castle was keeping a mystery from him, and this made him suspicious.

First, there was that business of the grandfather clock, broken for years. Parky had never managed to get it working, but then one morning it suddenly rang out as loud as a church bell. He hadn't fixed it, none of the other staff had, so how had it come suddenly back to life?

Then there were things like the books on the shelves – it wasn't that they had been moved, or were out of place. It was something else, something he alone could feel. It was almost as if they were being enjoyed again.

Same with the rooms: though they were spotless as always, they were somehow not as stale. Less like a museum, and more like a... like a home. Yes, that was it. Like a home. There was an almost imperceptible heartbeat running through the castle.

Parky couldn't quite place it. He didn't dare bring it up with the other staff; they would think he was cracked.

Could someone really be hiding here? Parky kept his thoughts to himself, and started doing a second round of the castle at the end of the day, to make sure the rooms were empty. He also began to lay traps.

\* \* \*

'There, see – stuck between the bottom of the door and the doorframe. That tiny slip of paper.'

It was evening, and the Duke and the twins were out and about.

'You're meant to open the door and the paper falls off unnoticed. An old trick to see if someone has been in your room. That crafty bounder has laid us a trap.'

'What's a bounder?' Stella asked. She carefully removed the slip of paper and made a note of where it had been stuck so she could put it back again.

'An ungentlemanly person, a conniving cad. That man Parkin.'

'The caretaker?'

'The very same.' The ghost began to pace the hall. 'Well, well, well, so old Parky suspects

33

something, does he? I was hoping it wouldn't come to this, but it was probably only a matter of time.'

'But we've been really, really careful to put everything back exactly the way it was. We haven't left a crumb on the carpet or a wrinkle in the bedspread.' Stella was puzzled. 'If anything, the castle is in better shape than when we first moved in.'

'I suspect that's the problem – Parkin knows this castle as well as I do. He can tell the mood of the place has changed. That new life has been breathed into her.' The Duke stopped pacing. 'It was a mistake to fix the clock. Blast it! I knew it at the time.'

The Duke tried to slap his hands together angrily but they went through each other and he stumbled off balance. Tom tried not to laugh. The Duke glared at him.

'This is no laughing matter. If Parkin finds you out, then you'll have to leave. And none of us want that now, do we?'

Tom's grin faded. 'So what do we do?'

'We must lie low and not set off any traps. I followed him around this afternoon, hidden in the walls and watched him lay at least four more.' The Duke thought for a moment. 'There are two more doors with slips of paper, one that has a book resting up against it on the inside, and he's even dusted the kitchen floor with a little flour to catch footprints.'

Tom whistled. 'Smart man. But why doesn't he just lie in wait for us?'

'If we trigger the traps, that will be his next move. We will have to be vigilant. Now, don't you two worry. As long as we're one step ahead of him, things should be alright.'

And with that, they settled down to watch The Simpsons and eat carrot cake.

# CHAPTER SIX

# Mrs Crank

Avoiding Parkin became something of a game, and it's fair to say that both teams found themselves enjoying it. Getting to the bottom of the mystery had enlivened the caretaker. He was almost certain now that someone was hiding in the castle and he would find them. He had noticed, however, that whoever it was, they were really looking after the place. In his mind, that made them competitors, rather than enemies.

The contest between the caretaker and the twins wasn't entirely fair as Stella and Tom had the advantage of having a ghost on their side, and the ghost of Britain's greatest ever soldier to boot. (If you'll excuse the pun.)

By sneaking about the castle undetected, Wellington was able to sniff out Parky's plans before the caretaker could put them into action: the decoy chocolates left on the dining table, tempting someone to take one; the single hairs stuck to the sides of drawers that would fall off if they were opened; the books placed carefully, left open on a specific page – waiting for someone to move the book or change the page by accident.

The twins avoided them all, but there were still a few close calls. These tended to happen outside in the grounds, where the Duke couldn't haunt.

One time the twins were lounging about in Leafage, their hut in the woods, not doing very much at all other than listening to the birds in the trees and the rustling of the leaves. Rarely did anyone ever enter this bit of the woods, since the tourists mostly stuck to the paths, so they generally felt safe there. But that afternoon they heard footsteps, dangerously close. Through the gaps in the hut, they could see Parkin clomping in their direction, rake in hand, looking at the hut, a perplexed look on his face. They were trapped.

But just when he was almost on top of the hut, Parky's walkie-talkie crackled to life and he turned back to the castle in a hurry. Stella and Tom quickly ducked out of the hut and ran the long way around the grounds, and sat in the Queen Mother's gardens, panting but relieved.

A few days later, when they went back into the woods they were surprised to see Leafage was still there. They had expected to see it broken into pieces. Not only was it not broken, inside the hut the floor had a new, thick carpet of leaves. Now it was the twins' turn to be puzzled.

But as it turned out, the twins didn't have to worry much longer about Parkin seeking them out. The caretaker soon had other, much more distressing things on his mind.

*** 

A smart-looking lady, as sharp as the creases in her suit, swept into the castle one morning with two assistants. They came direct from the head office of the company that ran the castle, and they did not bring good news.

'Call Mr Parkin if you please,' the lady said. (Though the way she said *please*, it was clear she didn't mean it.) 'Tell him Mrs Crank, Director of Marketing, is here to see him.' She fussed with her large hairdo that sat on top of her head like a beehive. It had taken Monsieur Rafael an hour to get it just right, and she wasn't going to let a single hair fall out of place. The train journey hadn't helped.

Soon after, Parky came running into the ticket office, he whipped off his gardening gloves and thrust out a large hand, red and sweaty at Mrs Crank[2].

'Sorry, I was just out in the compost pile.'

Mrs Crank stared at Parkin's hand, but declined to shake it.

'It's just that I wasn't expecting anyone from head office,' he went on.

'We've come unannounced.'

'To what do I owe the pleasure?' Parky smiled nervously. Visits from head office were rarely something to be cherished.

'We're here to turn this place around. It's been underperforming for years. We're here to make changes.'

'Underperforming? I'm afraid I don't understand what you mean,' said Parkin, puzzled.

---

[2] For those of you who don't know, a crank is a mechanical handle you can use to start an engine. It is also a rude way of calling someone a bit of an oddball. Funnily enough, both of these suited Mrs Crank. She was both cold and mechanical, *and* had bizarre ideas and plans. And you will soon learn what these were.

Now one of the assistants unrolled a large poster and stuck it up near the entrance to the ticket shop. 'Wellington Hotel Spa,' it read. 'Be treated like a Duke in historical surroundings. Massive Re-development. Coming Soon.'

Parkin read the words with horror. His eyes widened. He leaned on the ticket counter for support. 'I'm still not sure I understand,' he said.

'We're going to turn this old castle into a boutique spa and hotel,' said Mrs Crank. 'By the time we're through, you won't even recognise the place.' She gave a wide smile. 'It's going to be wonderful.'

***

Parky wasn't the only one in a state of shock. That night the Duke of Wellington lay on his campaign bed (or rather, lay half on, half in), recovering his composure. Stella and Tom were squeezed into the Duke's armchair.

'But they can't be serious. I've never heard such a ridiculous idea. It makes my blood run cold.' The duke thought for a moment. 'Well, it would if I had any blood.'

'What is a spa?' asked Tom.

'It's a place where ladies come to be pampered,'

41

said Stella. 'They get mud smeared on their faces and have bits of cucumber on their eyes. They walk around in towels a lot and people rub their feet.'

'It sounds absolutely ghastly,' said the Duke. 'This castle has been here for centuries and deserves better. I shan't have beastly sightseers occupying my rooms. This is my home, after all.'

'Our home too,' said Stella. 'But perhaps the time has come for us to give up the castle and go away. We've had a good run here.'

'Never! You're not going anywhere,' the Duke snapped. He wagged his finger at the twins. 'The hardest thing of all for a soldier is to retreat, and I don't intend to start now!'

Stella and Tom smiled at the old ghost. They had come to love his bluster and determination.

'First we must find out exactly what we're up against. This will require some strategy, some espionage.' The Duke was bursting with life. 'I'll start tomorrow!'

# CHAPTER SEVEN

# Verruca fish

Mrs Crank marched up the stairs, and a small group trotted behind her, struggling to keep up. There were the two assistants, Mr Pitt the architect, Jezzard the builder and, last of all, Parkin.

The ghost followed them, hidden inside the walls.

Mrs Crank stopped at the top of the staircase. 'Now this terrible blue colour will have to go – make a note, Jezzard. And all these stuffy old paintings on the walls will come down. Light and space is what this place needs, light and space.'

Parky's face was getting longer by the minute. This tour was depressing him.

'But that blue has been used for generations,' he argued. 'We spent a long time getting the match just perfect to preserve the history.'

Mrs Crank glared at him. 'As I keep having to tell you, this castle is no longer in the business of preserving history, Mr Parkin. It is in the business of making money. Light and space, don't you see?' She turned to Jezzard. 'Use Jasmine Blossom on this corridor, from top to bottom.'

Jezzard scribbled it down in his notebook. The assistants scribbled it down in theirs.

'Have you had any more thoughts on what you want to do with that poky little Wellington's room?' The architect gestured through the open doorway to the Duke's chambers.

'Ghastly, isn't it?' Mrs Crank sniffed. The architect nodded in agreement. 'And that awful wallpaper.' She turned to Parkin. 'Before the builders start you will see to it that all these effects are removed. They can be sent to a museum.' The assistants quickly jotted this down.

'But we *are* a museum, Mrs Crank,' pleaded Parkin.

'No, Mr Parkin, we are not,' snapped Mrs Crank. 'We are a hotel spa.' She nodded at the room. 'And this room here will be perfect for the Garra rufa fish.'

'The what?' asked Parky, knowing he didn't really want to hear the answer.

One of the assistants spoke up. 'Tanks of little fish. You put your feet in and they nibble them clean, it's the latest thing.'[3] She rolled her eyes at him. *These country types don't know anything*, she thought to herself.

'But the Duke of Wellington was our country's greatest military leader. When he died and his coffin was lying in this very room, almost ten thousand people came to pay their respects, they thought so much of him. We can't have it full of verruca fish, it wouldn't be right.'

Mrs Crank and her assistants wrinkled their noses simultaneously.

'You mean there was once a dead body in here?' said Mrs Crank. 'How awful. Just as well we're giving the place a total facelift.'

'I've just had an idea, Mrs Crank,' interrupted one of the assistants cheerfully. 'I see a slogan: "Feel like you've been on the march all day? Give foot ache the boot – the Wellington boot!" We could have his boots stuck on the wall.'

'Perfect,' said Mrs Crank. The assistants wrote it down.

---

[3] Yes, Garra rufa fish are real, and people pay money to have the little nippers eat the dead skin off their feet. Fun for the people, and a lovely snack for the Garra rufa fish.

Parkin felt sick. This couldn't be happening. The ghost himself was trembling with anger.

Mrs Crank turned and led the way up the stairs.

'Now, I want to have a look at the Lord Warden's apartments, or should I say, the Honeymoon Suite.'

In the apartments upstairs, the ghost burst through the wall. 'Hide!' he hissed at Stella and Tom. 'Quick, under the bed. Intruders!'

The twins scampered under the bed as quickly and quietly as they could. The Duke climbed through the wardrobe door.

A moment later Mrs Crank and her entourage clattered into the room. Stella and Tom watched the pairs of shoes nervously.

'Ah, this is more like it,' Mrs Crank said. She gave a wide sweep with her arms, then hurriedly checked to see that she hadn't upset her hairdo. 'Very grand. Very elegant.'

Parkin breathed a sigh of relief.

'This room can stay as it is, except for the curtains, the carpet, the furniture – and we'll have to knock down that wall there, won't we, Mr Pitt?'

'Yes, if we want to fit in the "his and hers" seaweed baths.'

Inside the wardrobe the Duke was reeling. So was Parkin.

'And surely this honeymoon suite will need one of them sauna things, and a place for a sunbed,' he said sarcastically.

'Don't be so silly, Mr Parkin,' snorted Mrs Crank. 'Those things will be going into the dungeon along with the gymnasium and the Ayurvedic treatment tables. We're going to call it the "Lower Mezzanine Pamper Suite".'

Parky sank onto the bed. The springs pushed down on Stella and Tom. They held their breath. 'The Lower Mezzanine Pamper Suite,' he repeated in a whisper. 'What's next?'

'I told you before, Mr Parkin,' tutted Mrs Crank, 'you'll hardly believe it's the same castle when we're through.'

'I'm just glad the Duke isn't around to see this,' said Parkin. 'It would break his heart.'

'Come, come, Mr Parkin, you're being overly sentimental. What's past is past. We must focus on the future. I'm sure Wellington would agree.'

\* \* \*

But of course the Duke of Wellington didn't agree. In fact, he was as far from agreeable as a ghost could possibly be. That night his shape practically crackled with annoyance. His eyes burned with fury. The twins had never seen him this way before.

'So, what's past is past, eh? Well, I'll show *her*. The past is very much alive!'

'So what's the plan?' asked Tom.

The Duke grinned mischievously. 'Well, I think a little bit of haunting to start with. I've been waiting a long time to act like the sorts of ghosts you read about in stories. You can't build a health club and turn this place upside down if the staff are too scared to work.'

'What can we do to help?' asked Stella.

'Just sit back and enjoy the show.' And the Duke winked.

# CHAPTER EIGHT

# Ghost hunter

The next day in her office, Mrs Crank was working hard at her desk. She glanced down at her watch. It was already lunchtime and she had only managed to approve half the architect's plans. It had been a busy morning, and her head ached something rotten.

She got out the little mirror and eye-liner from her handbag. *Better have a spruce-up*, she thought to herself.

Just as the eye-liner reached her face, out of the middle of her desk rose a silvery, human head. Right in front of her, as real as real could be, was the ghostly head of an old man, his sunken eyes closed, his cheeks sucked in, his skin transparent. Mrs Crank stopped still, the blood draining from her face.

The ghost slowly opened his dark eyes. 'Good morning,' he groaned at her through his teeth. Mrs Crank trembled. 'Tell me, have I come to the right place for a pampering?' the ghost moaned. Then he puffed out his cheeks and blew a gust of air through her hair.

The beehive toppled from her head. Mrs Crank shrieked at the top of her lungs, and jagged the eyeliner pencil across her face as her hands shook. She screamed, and waved her arms, and then screamed some more. Then she froze solid, her face went blank, and she crumpled into a heap on the desk.

Flump! Mrs Crank was out cold.

The Duke gave a little chuckle and sank back down into the furniture as the assistants came bursting into the room. *Rather good*, he thought to himself, *for a first go*.

After that the Duke quickly developed a real taste for spooking, and he threw himself into it wholeheartedly. He took to blending in with his marble bust, or holding the pose in one of his many portraits, and camouflaged like this, he'd lie in wait. He'd lurk till one of Crank's assistants or the architect, or the builder and his mate were walking the castle on their own, peacefully minding their own business. Then suddenly he'd turn his head and shout out something most bizarre at the top of his lungs, like 'Hogwash!' or 'Snickersnee!' The effect was horrifying.

Within the first few days of action, the Duke had caused two faintings. Not only were Crank's staff completely jittery, they sounded like utter fools saying that they had seen the ghost of the Duke of Wellington ('Yes, it was the Duke of Wellington!') and that the only thing he had said was 'Hogwash!'

Soon, everyone's nerves were on edge. Mrs Crank herself stayed away for two days, regaining her strength.

Then the twins joined the fight.

First, they went for Pitt the architect's measuring tools and plans. The twins didn't take them away – that would be stealing. They simply moved them from their usual place and left them somewhere else, just out of sight. This had the double effect of getting Pitt to waste time looking for his things, getting angrier by the minute, while also making him think he was losing his memory. Peeking out, the twins laughed to see him emptying his briefcase for the umpteenth time, hands on head. Pitt blamed the ghost.

Tom followed this up by applying the very nasty 'slugs-in-a-boot' tactic to the builders' boots, which they left on site. There is nothing quite as horrible as having a slug pop and squelch under your sock. It quite ruins your morning, as Jezzard and the builder's mate soon found out. They disliked this job already, and they hadn't even hammered a single nail. They too blamed the ghost.

Next, Stella took some cling film from the kitchen and spread a sheet of it tightly over some of the staff toilet bowls so that you couldn't even tell it was there. An invisible barrier. When the two assistants went to use the bathrooms on their break... well, you can just imagine. The two of them took a day off the next day. They blamed the ghost.

So between the Duke's haunting, and the children's pranks, little progress was made on turning the castle into a health retreat. The works ground to a halt. The Duke was as pleased as punch. Parky couldn't help but have a chuckle at Mrs Crank's expense. It hadn't escaped his attention that he and his team of castle keepers, as well as all the visitors, were being spared the ghostly treatment, and he thought he understood the reason why.

But you don't get to be someone like Mrs Crank by being weak-minded and giving up at the first sign of trouble. Back she came with vigour and determination. Monsieur Raphael had worked his magic with her hairdo, and it sat upon her head like the Rock of Gibraltar.

Mrs Crank was of the opinion that for every problem there was a solution. She hadn't believed in ghosts before, but if there was a ghost in the castle, so be it. There were ways of dealing with ghosts.

She gathered her team out in the castle gardens. They were a little puzzled as to why they were having a meeting out there, especially given that it was raining, but hiding underneath her umbrella, Mrs Crank explained.

'I've worked it out. That sneaky ghost has been eavesdropping on our plans. But I don't think he can hear us out here.' The others nodded. 'We must take him by surprise and then we can get on with our building work.'

'And how do you propose to do that?' asked Parkin. 'The Duke has probably been here for over a hundred and fifty years.'

'By calling in a ghost hunter, of course,' said Mrs Crank. 'One arrives next week. He comes highly recommended.' She grinned a terrible grin. 'His name is Seymour Stonyheart, and he's never failed to catch his prey yet.'

# CHAPTER NINE

# 'Up, Guards, and at 'em!'

It was evening, and the Duke and twins were playing indoor croquet. It would be more correct to say that Stella and Tom were playing croquet and the Duke was umpiring, as he couldn't hold a mallet. But, being a stickler for rules, he quite enjoyed the job. The twins had borrowed the mallets from the garden and were using rolled-up socks for balls. The legs of the tables and chairs were the hoops.

Tom was lining up a shot. It was a long one: from one end of the main drawing room, all the way under one of the chairs in the dining room. Get it and the game was his. Tom had to be careful that he didn't hit the sock ball too hard, or it might launch itself onto the dining table which was always set with glasses, cutlery and china.

'Come on, Tom,' said Stella. 'You're taking ages.'

'I have to agree,' said the Duke. 'I might have to mark you down for a penalty stroke.'

'You two just don't want me to win, but watch this!' Tom clattered the sock ball along the carpet. It bounced off the chair leg, and went into the fireplace.

'I win!' said Stella.

'Not fair,' grumbled Tom. 'You made me rush my shot.'

'Any longer on your shot and we would have been old and grey,' said the Duke. He looked down at his hands and body. 'Oops, too late,' he laughed, and the twins giggled at him.

The Duke caught sight of the clock. 'Goodness me, it's getting on. Put the things back as they were and straight upstairs.' The twins did as they were told.

They turned off all the lights and trooped upstairs, together with the Duke, who gave off enough of a glow for them to see where they were going.

They reached the door to the apartments, but strangely, there was bright light coming from underneath the door.

'I thought I told you to turn the lights off upstairs when we came down,' said the Duke.

'I did,' said Stella.

Looking at each other nervously, the twins pushed open the door – and froze. Inside, leaning back comfortably in one of the armchairs, was Parkin.

'What sort of time do you call this to be going to bed?' he said with a grin.

There was no escape. The game was well and truly up. So, hanging their heads a little (the Duke included), the three of them came in and plonked themselves on the bed, a feeling of dread washing over them.

'Don't worry, I'm not here to turf you out of the castle,' Parkin said, seeing the look on their faces. 'I'm here because I need your help.'

'But we thought you wanted us out,' said Tom.

Parkin nodded. 'I admit I did at first, but then I could see you weren't doing the castle any harm – if anything, things were a bit better round here, to be fair. Like that grandfather clock.'

'I knew fixing that clock would make you suspicious,' muttered the Duke.

Parkin turned to him. 'I'm here because I know you won't see this place turned into a hotel, and neither will I. But we've got a major problem on our hands.'

Parkin told them all about Stonyheart.

The twins' faces dropped. 'How on earth are we going to deal with both Mrs Crank and the ghost hunter?' asked Stella.

'By meeting them head-on in the field of battle,' snorted the Duke. 'I defeated Bonaparte, and now I'll defeat Stonyheart – it's as simple as that.'

'I don't think it will be all that straightforward,' said Parky. 'Apparently he's never lost yet. But if we put our heads together and work as a team, perhaps we can come up with a plan.'

The Duke thought for a moment then nodded. 'You're right, Mr Parkin, we are all in this together. Shall we unite forces and take on Crank and her allies?'

'Indeed we shall,' said Parky. 'Up, Guards, and at 'em!'

'Couldn't have put it better myself,' the Duke chuckled.

Even the twins managed a smile.

* * *

Seymour Stonyheart drove up the castle drive, the tyres of his van crunching the gravel. On the side of the van in cold, hard lettering was: 'Nuisance Control Services,' and underneath: 'Guaranteed'.

The van was otherwise plain, with blacked-out windows. On its roof there were aerials and satellite dishes of all sizes. This van looked like it meant business.

Stonyheart slid the van to a stop near the main drawbridge and climbed down. He was a small man, wiry and thin, with a face shaped like a clothes iron. He wore a black overcoat over a black suit, a black trilby hat over his black hair. His shoes were black, his socks were black. He looked completely gloomy, and that was because he was. There was no joy in this man, none whatsoever. The only thing he enjoyed was his job, and his job was capturing ghosts.

There are, broadly speaking, two types of people who deal with ghosts. One sort wear loose-fitting exotic clothing and have wonderful names like Madame Baboushka, or Augustus Mephisto Jr. They sometimes have crystal balls, or speak in funny voices, or ask the ghosts questions and then write down the answers in scribbly writing (ghosts always seem to have bad handwriting).

Then there are the others: the scientific ones who use expensive machines and computers. They set up infra-red cameras and wear headphones attached to special microphones. They have hand-held radars, and when they find a ghost, they trap them in tiny, electric force-field boxes and take them away. A decent ghost hunter will then release the ghost in the woods so he or she can carry on haunting in the wild – and most ghosts actually like a change of scene.

But though Seymour Stonyheart was scientific, he was certainly not one of the decent kind. He didn't see ghosts as having anything human about them at all. He never tried to find out why a ghost was haunting, or what could be done to allow the spirit to rest: he believed them to be nothing more than a foul pest that needed stamping out.

Stonyheart liked to keep the ghosts prisoners – trapped forever. He had a shelf of tiny force-field boxes in his van with the poor ghosts squashed inside, rather like trophies – the same way that ignorant, awful people once used to have tiger heads on walls.

*Yes*, thought Stonyheart, looking up at the stone walls of the castle. *Time to go trophy-hunting.*

# CHAPTER TEN

# Like a snake

Up in her office, Mrs Crank greeted Stonyheart with enthusiasm. The two of them eyed each other up, each sensing immediately that they were rather similar. Cold, business-like, no-nonsense. Mrs Crank thought Stonyheart looked rather dashing dressed all in black. Stonyheart was quite taken by the tremendous pile of hair on top of Crank's head. But they weren't here for pleasantries – that could come later. First they had a ghost to deal with.

'Now, tell me everything you know about this ghost, and where I might find it,' Stonyheart said, perching himself on one of the office chairs.

'He began appearing only recently,' began Mrs Crank.

'He?' Stonyheart asked.

'The Duke of Wellington.'

'Mrs Crank.' Stonyheart curled his lips into a thin smile. 'The Duke of Wellington has been dead since 1852. The apparition that is fouling these walls is nothing more than a messy collection of electro-magnetic energy. It is no more the Duke of Wellington than I am. Please refer to it as "it".'

'It certainly looks like him,' Mrs Crank argued weakly.

Stonyheart ignored her. 'When did the apparition first appear?'

'Once we had started work on redeveloping the castle.'

'Re-developing?'

'Yes, as a spa hotel.'

Stonyheart nodded approvingly. 'Much better than this stuffy castle. Good money to be had in that racket.'

'Precisely. But we haven't got very far at all. He – er – *it* has been interfering with the architect and the builder, and upsetting us all.'

'Where was it seen last?'

'I believe in the Wellington Museum room. It popped out of one of Wellington's boots and made my assistant come out in a rash.'

Stonyheart got to his feet. 'I shall fetch my tools, then I want you to show me.'

*  *  *

The museum room had been closed off to visitors.
A notice on the door simply said 'Closed for
Cleaning.'

Parkin had been summoned to open the glass
case which housed the Duke's things – his medals,
his uniforms, some letters. He stood at the back of
the room with Mrs Crank, shaking his head.

From his black bag, Stonyheart had taken out
an electrical meter, with a set of electrodes (like
the sort you see in programmes about hospitals).
He began attaching the white discs to the boots,
then ran the wires back to the meter, and plugged
them in. The dial on the meter immediately began
revolving.

'Aha! Yes, yes. These boots are charged. No
doubt about it.' Stonyheart cracked his knuckles.
'I'll just set this reading here – ' he clicked a button
on the meter ' – and now we have its signal.'

'What's that?' asked Parkin.

'The signal of the ghost. Each one has its own.
Now I can track it using this meter.'

*Interesting*, thought Parky to himself. *That might
come in handy.*

Stonyheart got to his feet.

'Now, where else has this foulness been sighted?'

'Come with me,' said Mrs Crank. 'But you will be discreet, won't you, Mr Stonyheart? It would spell the end of the hotel spa if it got round that the castle was having ghost problems.'

'I'll be secret, like a snake waiting to strike,' Stonyheart hissed.

Mrs Crank showed Stonyheart some of the portraits that the ghost had appeared from, the Turnerelli bust, and her office desk. All were tested using the meter. With each reading Stonyheart got more and more excited. Mrs Crank showed him the ladies' loos and told him about the phantom blockage.

This time the electrical meter didn't move at all. 'You definitely have a pest problem, Mrs Crank, all the places you have shown me so far have a ghost reading,' said Stonyheart. 'But it hasn't been anywhere near here. There's nothing here. That was caused by something else.'

Mrs Crank looked perplexed. Parkin looked at the floor.

'I can't wait to get started on this one,' said Stonyheart. 'I'll track it down and catch it. Then I'll shut it in a box.'

'So you can help us?' asked Mrs Crank.

Stonyheart took her by the hand. 'Mrs Crank, not only can I help you – it will be a pleasure.' He smoothed down his hair. 'I don't think you have to worry. I've found in the past that ghosts are actually afraid of me. The horrible things know danger when it comes.' He sneered. 'Have your man here – ' he waved at Parkin ' – help me with my equipment. I'll start first thing in the morning.'

Parkin trudged down to the van behind Stonyheart. He was really beginning to dislike this man, with his silly black hat and overcoat.

The ghost hunter slid back the side door to reveal a compact little workshop. There was a desk with a computer and chair, and shelves of equipment: cables, microphones, cameras. There was also a shelf of black boxes – well over a dozen of them, all plugged in to a giant battery. Each of the boxes had a flashing red light on the top.

'What are those?' asked Parkin.

Stonyheart grinned proudly. 'Those are all the ghosts I've caught so far this year. I have more at home. Loads of them.'

'What happens if the boxes get unplugged and the lights go off?' asked Parkin.

'The boxes eventually run out of battery power, then wham!' Stonyheart clapped his hands

together. 'The ghosts escape like rats from a trap and we have mayhem on our hands. Imagine what it would be like with multiple ghosts running about the place. I never, ever unplug them.'

*Interesting*, thought Parkin again.

He helped Stonyheart carry his equipment inside. The duke, the twins and he would have to have another meeting this evening.

# CHAPTER ELEVEN

# A wild-ghost chase

The next morning, Mrs Crank decided to close the castle to visitors, and sent all the staff home. She didn't want word of the ghost hunt getting out.

Quite a few tourists were turned away. Having come down to the seaside especially, they were a little annoyed. They stood outside scratching their heads.

Encouraged by the news that the ghost was soon to be no more, the builder and the architect had both agreed to come back to work. They were busy measuring up rooms and marking out changes.

The two assistants were busy too, drawing up advertising slogans, and spa treatment menus. (£145 for the Indian rope massage, £162 for a course of hot stones and so on. Ridiculous, if you ask me.)

Mrs Crank was in her office making phone calls.

Stonyheart had laid out all his equipment. He had placed empty force-field boxes in several of the rooms, and had attached them to a battery. There were cables running all over the place, microphones on stands, motion-sensing cameras. He got out his meter and flicked it on. The meter crackled into life and the dial started spinning. The ghost was nearby. Stonyheart licked his lips. Time to get started.

Though Stonyheart didn't know it, Parkin had told the Duke and the twins about the meter, and how it worked. Together they had laid a trail for the ghost hunter. The ghost hunter was going to go on a bit of a wild-goose chase, or rather a wild-ghost chase. While he was distracted, they would put the rest of the plan into action.

So the night before, the Duke of Wellington had rolled himself along certain carpets to leave as much of his signal as possible. Stella and Tom had borrowed some things from the gift shop and had thrown them back and forth through his body. (The Duke didn't care for that at all.) Then the things had been put back where they found them. They had done the same with bits and pieces from the kitchen.

The Duke and the twins would stay out of sight until it was time for them to join the battle. 'Just like the reverse slope defence, you know,' he chortled. 'Keep the troops out of sight and draw the enemy in. Hurrah!'

So it was no wonder that Stonyheart's dial was spinning furiously and his headphones were crackling. The trap had been set.

*Just you wait, ghostie, I'm on to you*, Stonyheart thought.

He crept down the corridor, meter in one hand, microphone in the other. There was a massive signal coming from the carpet. It was heading down the stairs, away from the stately rooms and towards the courtyard where the gift shop and café were. Stonyheart carried onwards.

\* \* \*

While the ghost hunter was busy on the trail, the twins were waiting. They were safely hidden in Leafage, with one of Parkin's walkie-talkies, waiting for the word to spring into action.

The walkie-talkie buzzed to life. 'All clear,' Parkin said. 'He's busy on the trail.'

'Let's go,' said Tom. The twins quickly crawled out of the hut and ran through the woods towards the fence and the car park. There they spotted the black van with the black windows. They ran up to it. As Parkin had suggested, the sliding door had been left unlocked.

'That's careless of him,' giggled Stella. She was beginning to enjoy herself.

Making sure no-one was looking, they slid open the door and crept inside. The boxes were there the way Parkin had said they would be, red lights blinking in the gloom.

'Which ones do we take?' said Tom. He lifted a couple of the boxes to see how heavy they were. 'I reckon I could manage two of them.'

Stella was peering closely at the boxes. They had labels on them but it was too gloomy to read them. 'I don't know, let's just grab a couple each and hope for the best.'

Nervously, they unplugged the boxes and got down from the van. They would get them back to the castle, then the Duke would take charge.

* * *

Stonyheart was in the kitchen. His meter was sending him all over the place: underneath tables, into the carrots in the larder, the pies in the chiller room, the pots and pans.

71

*This is one strange ghost*, thought Stonyheart. *Clearly likes its food*. He had never known ghosts to eat before.

Now he began to pick up a trail, leading to the gift shop. 'We'll soon have you, parasite!' he hissed.

The Duke, of course, was nowhere near either the kitchen or the gift shop. He had just emerged from the wardrobe in the apartments upstairs, ready for action. Stella and Tom had managed to sneak back inside the castle thanks to Parkin, and had brought the ghost boxes with them.

They laid them down on the carpet in front of the Duke and inched away, nervously. Parkin quickly pressed the release buttons. He stepped back and put a protecting arm around the twins.

The Duke nodded at them, then puffed up his chest, ready to assume command. The boxes began to beep, the red lights flashed faster and faster. There was a hiss and a puff of steam, then one by one, the boxes sprung open releasing their occupants.

# CHAPTER TWELVE

# 'Get what's coming to you!'

A Roman legionary in full battle armour burst into the room, half a dozen arrows buried in his back. (No question how he had died.) Behind him came a belly dancer in a glittering top and sequined skirt. They both began chattering excitedly and moving about the room, completely bewildered, the belly dancer jiggling and twirling.

The Duke tried to introduce himself. Stella and Tom clutched Parkin.

The doors to the third box swung open and a man in red and white football kit leapt into the room, football at his feet. He dribbled neatly around Stella and Tom and blasted a searing drive, raising his arms as he watched the ball soar into a goal only he could see. Another ghostly ball appeared magically at his boots.

'Anyone know where the other team is?' he asked peering about the room, then seeing the other ghosts, he joined in, making a loud racket. (Well, you would make a racket too, if you had been shut up in a container the size of a shoe box.)

None of them knew what was going on, especially the legionary, who was babbling at everyone in Latin.

Finally, the last box ran out of power. Out came a man wearing a suit and a black gown, with a pair

of spectacles perched on his nose. He carried a cane which he started swishing through the air. A ghostly headmaster.

'Now, where is that horrible little man?' roared the headmaster, looking around the room. 'He's going to get six of the best from my cane for locking me in that box.'

'Good show,' said the Duke, but he could barely be heard over the noise. He tried to get all the ghosts to stand still.

Finally he shouted, 'Attention!' and suddenly, there was silence. His voice carried such authority that, even after all these years of being a ghost, all the other ghosts stopped and stood in a line, even the belly dancer, who was just getting warmed up.

The Duke eyed each of them. 'Now I'm sure all of you have questions, and are completely in the dark as to what is going on, but I'm afraid there just isn't time for explanations. There will be plenty of opportunity for that later. But I'm sure you will agree that you want to get back at the man who trapped you.' The Duke pointed to one of the force-field boxes and mimed so that the legionary would understand The ghosts all nodded.

'And you agree that you much prefer being free, don't you?' Again the ghosts said yes.

The Duke began pacing back and forth, his arms behind his back. 'If you do as I tell you, you can have your revenge and your freedom before the day is out.'

The Duke stopped in front of each one to see that they were ready to follow orders. The ghosts were standing to attention, eyes front. 'Good. Now, here is what I want you to do...'

\* \* \*

Jezzard the builder was hunched over in the dining room over his building plans, making adjustments to his measurements, punching numbers into a calculator, working out just how he was going to fit a giant Jacuzzi into the room.

His day was about to be ruined.

'What's this?' a voice roared behind him. Jezzard leapt to his feet, heart beating wildly. In front of him stood a ghost. It looked like a headmaster, tapping a cane on his palm with purpose.

'Here we go again,' Jezzard groaned. He covered his eyes, hoping the ghost would go away. It didn't.

'Using a calculator in exams?' the headmaster bellowed. 'Cheating, were we?'

Jezzard stood frozen. He barely managed to speak.

'Er, n-n-o sir, I was just trying to – '

'*Silence!*' the headmaster cut in. Jezzard yelped in fright. 'Come here, boy, and get what's coming to you!'

The ghost advanced on the poor builder. From down the corridor all you could hear was a cane whistling through the air, and a scream.

Down in the dungeon, Pitt the architect was cowering in a corner, trying to hide behind his briefcase. Unless his eyes were playing tricks, in front of him was a centre forward – a dead centre forward. The man looked angry and dangerous, and clearly meant business.

'Stand up and defend!' shouted the footballer. He fired a shot and sent the ball whizzing just past the architect's nose. Pitt started to babble. 'No guts eh?' snarled the centre forward. 'We'll see about that.'

Up in the courtyard all you could hear was the thumping of football after football, and a long, desperate howl.

In the staffroom both the assistants were petrified – as still as statues. But it wasn't anything to do with toilets of mystery or the Duke of Wellington this time. There in front of them was another ghost. A soldier, with a shield, a sword, a spear and a bunch of arrows buried in his back. And he was gibbering at them in Latin.

'*Recedite, plebes! Gero rem imperialem*!'[4] the ghost shouted. '*Recedite, plebes!*'

The assistants didn't need to know Latin to know they needed to be somewhere else. Right away. Keeping an eye on the legionary, they began shuffling towards the door, trembling like leaves.

---

[4] 'Stand aside, little people! I am here on official business!'

They reached the doorway, the soldier still jabbering away at them, and broke into a run. All you could hear upstairs was their terrified wailing, followed by the clanking of armour.

* * *

Staring out from behind the curtains in their apartment upstairs, the twins were giggling furiously. The Duke was chuckling too.

Running across the lawn towards the car park, arms flapping, were Jezzard the builder, Pitt the architect, and the two assistants. They couldn't get to their cars fast enough. The cars lurched into life and soon were speeding down the driveway, sending up a shower of gravel.

Now there were only two adversaries left: Mrs Crank and Stonyheart. The Duke had saved the worst for last.

He nodded to Parkin. 'It's time to call Stonyheart. I believe Mrs Crank should be about ready.'

# CHAPTER THIRTEEN

## Stonyheart meets his Waterloo

Nearly every item in the gift shop lay scattered over the floor. There were books and tea mugs, stuffed toys and model catapult kits. Stonyheart had pulled apart the shop in desperation.

'Where is this trail going?' he muttered angrily. The ghost had to be near here. Its signal couldn't have been stronger had it been rubbing itself over the things in the gift shop.

Parkin ran into the room.

'Come quick, Mr Stonyheart!' He pointed upstairs.

'Is it the ghost?' asked Stonyheart greedily. 'Has it shown its face?'

Parkin shook his head. 'No, it's not the Duke,

it's Mrs Crank. Come with me, I think she might be possessed!'

Stonyheart dropped what he was doing and quickly followed the caretaker up to Mrs Crank's office. What on earth was going on now?

Parkin threw open the doors. 'See?'

Stonyheart was flabbergasted. He leaned on the wall for support.

Mrs Crank was belly dancing, her beehive bobbing and spinning to the sound of music no one else could hear. She twirled about the room, a smile glued to her face, her arms above her head, her hips swaying to and fro, her belly wobbling.

'I've waited so long to be free,' she cooed. Though it really didn't sound like Mrs Crank's voice at all. 'All these years I've been wanting to dance!'

Now she whirled even faster, shimmying up and down the office. A mad frenzy of dance, her body not her own.

Stonyheart's eyes were wide, his mouth hung open. 'Wait here, Parkin, while I get my electrodes,' he said in a whisper.

'But you mustn't leave!' trilled Mrs Crank. 'The show has just begun!'

She tried to grab Stonyheart's hand, but he snatched it back and left the room in a hurry.

When Stonyheart came back with his meter and his electrodes, Mrs Crank's hair had fallen around her shoulders in a wild mess, her face was flushed and she was swinging her head around and around, hair flying as she pranced around the room.

Stonyheart chased after her. 'Hold her, Parkin!' he shouted. 'We must get a reading.'

Parkin tried to corner Mrs Crank, but she skipped past him, arms twirling. Stonyheart managed to grab hold of her with one hand and Parkin came over to help.

Stonyheart started sticking electrodes onto her face. 'Not to worry, Mrs Crank, we'll soon get that horrible ghost out of you.'

'But I want to dance,' said Mrs Crank. 'I want to boogie!'

'No, you don't, Mrs Crank, this isn't you talking. It's some terrible vermin that's got hold of you.'

'If anyone's vermin around here, it's *you*, Stonyheart!' boomed a voice from the doorway.

Stonyheart spun round to see a silvery shape hovering in the doorway. It was the shape of a man, strong and proud. His arms were folded, and he glared at Stonyheart along a fierce nose.

Stonyheart took a step back. He looked at Mrs Crank and then back at the Duke. Were there two ghosts? What was going on? He pressed himself up against the wall.

'You may come out now, madam,' said the Duke to Mrs Crank.

'Oh, do I have to?' said a voice from inside Mrs Crank. 'I'm having such fun.'

Stonyheart watched in amazement as Mrs Crank

gave a sudden shudder, and out wriggled the ghost of a lady in a dazzling costume, a ruby in her bellybutton. The ghost curtsied to him with a smile.

Mrs Crank flopped into a chair, exhausted from all her efforts. She was too confused to speak and just crumpled into a heap.

The ghost floated away happily and joined the Duke.

'You're an excellent dancer, madam. First rate,' said the Duke beaming at her. 'Now, would you be so kind as to get the others?'

'Others?' yelled Stonyheart. 'There are *others*?'

'Oh yes,' said the Duke. 'I have quite a force. And you,' he grinned at Stonyheart, 'have just met your Waterloo.'

* * *

Stonyheart and Mrs Crank were slumped on chairs, pinned behind the desk. They were totally outnumbered. A circle of ghosts stood around them: an angry-looking headmaster, a footballer, a Roman legionary and the belly dancer, who was smiling at Mrs Crank.

Stonyheart recognised the ghosts as ones he had captured in other parts of the country. But how had they escaped? His head spun.

The Duke was talking to Mrs Crank. The director of marketing was slowly recovering from her shock at having been possessed by a dancing fiend. She peered out from behind a tangle of hair. Her face had lost all its earlier colour.

'This hotel-spa idea you have planned really isn't acceptable,' the Duke was saying. 'There is over five centuries of history here, you see.'

'I tried to tell you,' said Parkin. 'Neither his Grace here nor I will see this place turned into mud baths.'

Mrs Crank nodded weakly. 'So you're in this together?'

'I'm afraid so, Mrs Crank, yes,' said Parkin.

'Traitor!' hissed Stonyheart.

The legionary banged his sword against his shield, the headmaster swung his cane, and Stonyheart sunk back in his chair.

Mrs Crank looked at the ghostly quartet surrounding her.

'And where did *they* come from?' Her bottom lip quivered. 'There used to be only you.'

'From Stonyheart's van – we set them free. These ghosts are under my command,' the Duke said proudly.

Parkin laughed. 'Faced with our new ghosts,

Pitt, Jezzard and your two assistants ran away earlier, and I doubt they will return.'

'And even if they were to somehow come back,' added the Duke, 'and you do renovate my castle, I must warn you as soon as the first customer sets foot in the hotel, we ghosts will make sure their visit is cut short, if you catch my meaning.' He guffawed.

'Then there really is no hope for the Wellington Spa now, is there?' Mrs Crank said wearily.

'Absolutely none,' replied the Duke.

'Then I give up,' said Mrs Crank. She took out her handkerchief and dabbed at her eyes. 'You win. You can have your castle back.'

She turned to Stonyheart. 'It seems your services will no longer be required. You're dismissed.'

# CHAPTER FOURTEEN

# Things turn out well

Stonyheart leapt to his feet, and bravely made a dash for the door, barging his way through the ghosts. He wiped at his clothes with a disgusted look on his face as if they had been rolled in mud, and glared around the room, his eyes crazed.

His voice rose in pitch as he shouted at them all.

'Mrs Crank may be giving up, but I certainly haven't!'

Parkin and the Duke moved away from him.

'I hate ghosts, do you hear!' Stonyheart was practically foaming at the mouth. 'I hate the lot of you, and now I know where you are, I'll be coming back. Just you wait!'

He ran from the room laughing like a maniac, and fled from the castle, picking up his equipment as he went, and hauling it to his van in a jumble.

'What a strange man,' said the Duke. 'I'm rather glad to be rid of him.'

He turned to the other ghosts. 'Job well done, you're dismissed for the day. Find a comfortable place to hide and we'll meet later. And no further spooking of humans unless ordered,' he added.

The ghosts happily vanished into the walls.

Parkin smiled at Mrs Crank kindly. 'There's still quite a few tourists outside, what say we straighten this place out and let them in? I would hate for us to lose the ticket money.'

Mrs Crank sighed. 'But how can we open up with just the two of us? I sent all the staff home.'

'Ah,' said Parkin, 'I have an idea there. Hold on.' He pulled his walkie-talkie off his belt. 'Parkin here. The coast is clear, come down to the office.' Mrs Crank looked at him, puzzled. 'My new assistants,' Parkin said with a grin.

Stella and Tom had been in hiding, waiting to hear the outcome of the battle. As soon as they received the call they rushed downstairs. They slowed down as they got to the office door, not quite sure what to expect.

'Ah, here you are,' the Duke said when the twins had poked their heads round the door. 'Come to save the day.'

The twins still had no idea what was going on, and stood there silently, a bit worried to be out in the open after all these weeks of hiding.

Parkin came over and took them gently by the arms. 'This is Stella, and this is Tom. My trainee castle wardens. They just happened to be doing some work for me in the castle grounds – weren't you?' Parkin slipped them a wink.

Tom was confused for a second, then he twigged. 'Yes, of course,' he nodded, smiling. 'Working in the grounds. Trainee wardens. Pleased to meet you.' He shook Mrs Crank's hand.

'We were weeding in the moat,' Stella added.

Mrs Crank looked them up and down. They seemed rather young to be working as wardens, but after the events of today, nothing about this castle would surprise her any more.

'Very well. Give me a moment to fix my hair, Mr Parkin.' She nodded at Stella and Tom. 'And you two, come with me. We have a ticket office to run.'

'That's the spirit,' laughed the Duke. 'I mean spirit as in enthusiasm, not spirit as in ghost,' he added, winking at Mrs Crank.

She glared back at him. 'Don't you have a cupboard you should be hiding in?'

It turned out to be a busy day with a constant stream of tourists. Stella and Tom coped well. They quickly tidied up the shop, and were good about taking money for tickets and giving out the right change.

Mrs Crank was very happy to see the work done and the money coming in. Parkin suggested that the twins could keep on helping out, and she said that was entirely up to him. And when she asked them where they lived, Parkin interrupted to say, 'They're staying with me at the castle, till they find their own place.'

Mrs Crank just nodded and didn't ask any awkward questions. As far as she was concerned, Parkin was dealing with the ghosts, and if he wanted his trainee wardens to help out, she wasn't going to make trouble. In fact, she was quite exhausted from the most amazing dance workout she'd ever had, and she was wondering if the belly dancing ghost would offer regular sessions for a few select clients. The Strictly Spirits Dance Studio sounded good...

Later that night after Mrs Crank had gone home and the castle was locked up, the twins, Parkin and

the Duke were lounging about in the apartment, eating takeaway pizza. (Well, the Duke wasn't eating, of course.)

'First a home and now jobs,' whistled Tom. 'Things have turned out well.'

'But it's not all going to be Simpsons and carrot cake around here. There'll be lots of reading and maths for homework,' said the Duke. The twins groaned.

'Do you think that horrible man Stonyheart will come back like he said he would?' asked Tom. 'Aren't you worried?'

'I wouldn't give him too much thought,' Stella said with a giggle. She had a mischievous look on her face. 'Something tells me he's probably in a bit of a pickle.'

* * *

Seymour Stonyheart sped away from the castle, fuming. Never before had a ghost got the better of him. Never before had he failed. That woman Crank was weak. How dare she give up on him? He would have his revenge, oh yes!

Stonyheart was so cross as he drove, and was grinding his teeth together so loudly, that he failed to notice that in the back of the van, the lights on top of all the ghost boxes had begun to blink. The boxes were unplugged and slowly losing power. In fact they only had about a minute's worth of power left. After that the lids would spring open.

Seymour Stonyheart drove on, and behind him, a dozen angry apparitions waited for their chance to burst free.

# A Note from the Author

The story, characters and events of this book are all fictional, but the unnamed castle in my story looks rather like Walmer Castle, a real place that you can visit. I borrowed some real details from this wonderful building for my fictional castle, such as the ramparts and cannons, the gardens and woods, the apples called Newton Wonders, the Duke of Wellington's room with its campaign bed, the museum with his boots, and many more things besides.

I love visiting Walmer Castle with my family. The idea of children living a secret life in a castle like it came from my daughter Mia.

Luckily, unlike the castle in my story, Walmer Castle is run by English Heritage, a wonderful organisation that protects historic places from people like Mrs Crank, so that future generations can understand and enjoy our past.

Though the character of the Duke of Wellington in this story is obviously made up, lots of the historical details are true. The real Duke of Wellington did battle with Tipu Sultan, the ruler of the kingdom of Mysore in 1799. He lived in Walmer Castle, thinking it was 'the most charming marine residence'. When he died in 1852, over nine thousand people came to the castle to pay their respects to Britain's greatest ever soldier.

Even three of the things my ghost says in the story are the Duke of Wellington's real words (or thought to be).

'The whole art of war consists in getting at what is on the other side of the hill.'

'The hardest thing of all for a soldier is to retreat.'

'Up, Guards, and at 'em!'

## And finally...

Though Wellington was well known for being a strict leader and a tough soldier, he was often kind to children, and in my story I tried to bring that side of his character out a bit.

A well-known yarn about the Duke, which I like to believe might be true, tells of a time when he was out on a walk and came across a young boy who was crying. Wellington asked what was wrong, and the boy replied that he was sad because he had to go back to boarding school the next day and wasn't able to take his pet toad. To cheer the boy up, the Duke took the toad and promised to look after it.

A few weeks later the boy received a letter. It said: 'Field Marshal the Duke of Wellington presents his compliments to Master – – , and has the pleasure to inform him that his toad is well.'

Fancy that.